Agatha
Girl of Mystery

GROSSET & DUNLAP
Published by the Penguin Group
Penguin Group (USA) Inc., 375 Hudson Street, New York, New York 10014, USA
Penguin Group (Canada), 90 Eglinton Avenue East, Suite 700, Toronto, Ontario M4P 2Y3, Canada
(a division of Pearson Penguin Canada Inc.)
Penguin Books Ltd, 80 Strand, London WC2R 0RL, England
Penguin Ireland, 25 St. Stephen's Green, Dublin 2, Ireland (a division of Penguin Books Ltd)
Penguin Group (Australia), 707 Collins Street, Melbourne, Victoria 3008, Australia
(a division of Pearson Australia Group Pty Ltd)
Penguin Books India Pvt Ltd, 11 Community Center, Panchsheel Park, New Delhi—110 017, India
Penguin Group (NZ), 67 Apollo Drive, Rosedale, Auckland 0632, New Zealand
(a division of Pearson New Zealand Ltd)
Penguin Books, Rosebank Office Park, 181 Jan Smuts Avenue, Parktown North 2193, South Africa
Penguin Books, Rosebank Office Park, 181 Jan Smuts Avenue, Parktown North 2193, South Africa
Penguin China, B7 Jaiming Center, 27 East Third Ring Road North, Chaoyang District, Beijing 100020, China

Penguin Books Ltd, Registered Offices: 80 Strand, London WC2R 0RL, England

Original Title: Agatha Mistery: L'enigma del faraone
Text by Sir Steve Stevenson
Original cover and illustrations by Stefano Turconi

English language edition copyright © 2013 Penguin Group (USA) Inc. Original edition published by Istituto Geografico De Agostini S.p.A., Italy, 2010. © 2010 Atlantyca Dreamfarm s.r.l., Italy

International Rights – Atlantyca S.p.A. – via Leopardi 8, 20123 Milano, Italia
foreignrights@atlantyca.it – www.atlantyca.com

Published in 2013 by Grosset & Dunlap, a division of Penguin Young Readers Group, 345 Hudson Street, New York, New York 10014. GROSSET & DUNLAP is a trademark of Penguin Group (USA) Inc. Printed in the U.S.A.

Library of Congress Cataloging-in-Publication Data is available.

10 9 8 7 6 5 4 3 2 1

ISBN 978-0-448-46217-2

PEARSON

ALWAYS LEARNING

Agatha

Girl of Mystery

The Curse of the Pharaoh

by Sir Steve Stevenson
illustrated by Stefano Turconi

translated by Siobhan Kelly
adapted by Maya Gold

Grosset & Dunlap
An Imprint of Penguin Group (USA) Inc.

FIRST MISSION
Agents

Agatha
Twelve years old, an aspiring mystery writer; has a formidable memory

Dash
Student at the prestigious private school, Eye International Detective Academy

Chandler
Butler and former boxer with
impeccable British style

Watson
Obnoxious Siberian cat with
the nose of a bloodhound

Aunt Patricia
Lives in a lavish Luxor villa . . .
and breeds camels!

DESTINATION

Egypt: Valley of the Kings

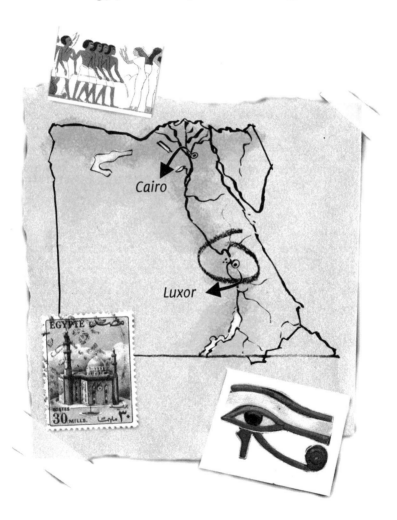

OBJECTIVE

To discover who stole an ancient artifact from an archaeological dig in the Valley of the Kings—where the sun sets and the pharaohs have slept in their tombs for thousands of years. And beware of Tutankhamen's curse.

The Investigation Begins...

The penthouse sat high atop of Baker Palace, fifteen floors above street level. Its roof was covered with state-of-the-art solar panels, and if you stood on the wraparound terrace and peered in through the tinted-glass windows, the first thing you'd see was a mass of high-tech electronics—monitors, Wi-Fi antennas, and routers—surrounded by pizza boxes, fast-food bags, and dirty socks.

The only person at home was a lanky fourteen-year-old boy, sprawled out snoring on the couch with his dark hair flopped over his face. He had left his seven computers on all night long,

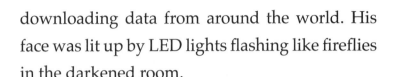

downloading data from around the world. His face was lit up by LED lights flashing like fireflies in the darkened room.

Outside the penthouse London, England, was already bathed in a milky haze. It had been a sweltering summer, too hot for tourists, and the Thames River looked like a strip of shiny tar.

Not far from Baker Palace, the famous Big Ben clock tower chimes struck six times. The low

notes rattled the walls, but Dashiell Mistery slept like a rock.

Dash was not a morning person. He liked lazing around the penthouse all day and never started his homework till late at night, usually with the music cranked. His report cards said it all: Dash was getting straight As in Surveillance Technologies, but he was flunking everything else.

"Instead of going to that crazy detective school, why don't you study engineering?" his mother would beg on the rare occasions when they had a real conversation. "The Mistery family could use a few people with practical skills." Dash shrugged and said, "Don't forget Grandpa Ellery, Mom. He's at CERN in Geneva studying subatomic particles. That's pretty hardcore." And the conversation would end with his mom sighing, "He's a nuclear physicist, not a normal engineer. All you Mistery men have to do something different!"

Dash secretly liked being known as a "Mistery man." After her divorce, his mother never missed a chance to label the Mistery family a pack of oddballs. First and foremost was her ex-husband, Edgar Allan Mistery, a champion curler. (Curling is an Olympic sport played with brooms and polished rocks on an ice rink; it isn't exactly

mainstream.) Every one of Edgar's relatives was part of her roll call of hopeless eccentrics.

6:15 a.m.: Second wake-up attempt. The words RED ALERT flashed on a monitor screen, accompanied by the theme from *Star Trek*, and a metallic voice that kept repeating, "Man the lifeboats!"

This time around, Dash's forehead was targeted by a laser-tag strobe light. The room looked like the bridge of an alien spaceship.

But it was no use: Dash just rolled over and buried his head in the pillow. Within seconds, he was out like a light.

6:30 a.m.: Final attempt. First the phone rang several times. Then the automatic blinds rolled up, buzzing, while a wall of speakers blasted the latest hit.

A neighbor banged on the door, yelling, "This isn't a nightclub, you slacker!"

Still nothing.

Finally at precisely 6:36 a.m., in the middle of all the deafening chaos, there was a tiny *blip*. It came from a titanium gadget, shaped like a cell phone, which hung from a charger cord over the couch.

That faint *blip* rang in Dash's ears like a volley of gunfire. Without getting up, he reached out, grabbed the gadget, and pressed a few buttons.

A dreadful message flashed onto the screen.

The second that Dash read it, his eyes bulged. "Today?" he yelled. "There's absolutely no way!"

He jumped to his feet. This was a total disaster. He grabbed various remotes, clicking off the alarms, ringtones, and speakers. "There's no time to sort all this out. I have to . . . I have to . . . what do I have to do?!" he exclaimed.

He perched on the arm of a chair, quickly booting up his seven computers, which came to life with a flash of white light. "I'll email Agatha!"

he said aloud. "But will she read it in time?" He checked the gadget again, with a grimace. "No, better not. If they hack into my email, it's all over."

Where did he put that cordless phone? He found it under a burger wrapper. Feverishly he scrolled through his contacts, "Adam, Adrian . . . Agatha! Got it!"

He started to text her, but stopped. What if they'd put a bug on his phone? They were experts at stuff like that!

"Okay, don't panic, Dash," he whispered. "Concentrate. What's the best way to get a message to Agatha without anyone listening in?" He ran a hand through his floppy hair and made a decision.

Dash stepped onto the terrace, unlatched the door to his aviary, and grabbed his trusty carrier pigeon. "Time to put you to work, buddy. The Mistery Cousins need you!"

Those Eccentric Misterys

$\mathcal{A}$s the pigeon soared over the suburbs of London, the patchwork of roofs and yards gave way to a wide swath of green: three acres of flowering meadows, fountains, lily ponds, botanical gardens, and quiet, leafy lanes.

Smack in the middle of the park was a Victorian mansion with a lavender roof: the Mistery Estate, home of twelve-year-old Agatha Mistery and her parents.

Agatha was taking a morning stroll in her slippers and bathrobe, dodging the rotating jets of the sprinkler system. The scent of freshly mowed

grass tickled her nose—her small, upturned nose, a Mistery family trait.

She carried a cup of steaming tea, which she savored in tiny sips. It was top-quality Shui-Hsien, with a scent like honey and a fruity aftertaste. In a word: superb.

She followed the path to a gazebo, where she sat on a purple swing, resting her teacup next to a pile of letters. Mostly junk mail, bills, and silly postcards from friends on vacation. Agatha didn't bother to read them.

Then she noticed a package on the table. It was covered with stamps, postmarks, and labels from several countries.

What could it be?

"Chandler?" called Agatha.

The Mistery Estate's trusty butler peered out from behind a hydrangea bush, armed with a pair of gardening shears. He was pruning stray

twigs, dressed in an extra-large black tuxedo that seemed more suited to a gala event than a garden. An ancient straw hat perched on top of his head.

"Good morning, Miss Agatha." Chandler waved his shears and gave her what passed for a smile, a very faint crack in the great slab of his face. A former professional boxer, he was known for his stony expression.

"What's this?" asked Agatha, picking up the mysterious package. "Where did it come from?"

"From the Andes, Miss Agatha."

"Then it's from Mom and Daddy!"

Agatha crossed her legs and started unwrapping the package, carefully noting the sequence of stamps. "This first one is the postmark of Laguna Negra in Peru," she said aloud. "They're there right now, at thirteen thousand feet above sea level!"

"Just so, Miss."

"And then the post office in Ica, the Andean province," she said, concentrating. "Then Lima, the capital of Peru, then . . . that's strange! Do you see that?"

"Do I see what, Miss Agatha?"

"This stamp, right under the air-mail sticker." Agatha chewed her lip. "It says Mexico City."

Chandler nodded.

"And finally the last stage: from Mexico City to London, endorsed at Heathrow Airport!" She took the last sip of her Shui-Hsien, then pulled her trusty notebook from her pocket and opened it to a blank page. She clicked open her favorite pen, but the ink had gone dry. Frowning, she scribbled a bit, leaving dents in the paper. "Have you got a pen?" she asked Chandler.

Agatha never missed a chance to take notes on an interesting detail. Like every member of the Mistery family, she had her heart set on an eccentric career.

She wanted to be a mystery writer.

And not just *any* mystery writer: the best in the world! To train her prodigious memory, she took notes constantly, read encyclopedia entries for fun, and traveled to every corner of the planet whenever she got the chance. She prided herself on her attention to detail.

"A pen?" she asked again.

The butler stood looking at her.

"Is something wrong, Chandler?"

He pulled a gold pen from his tuxedo jacket and passed it to her with a little cough. "Not to put too fine a point on it," he said, "but don't you plan to open your birthday present, Miss Agatha?"

"Of course, silly me!" She ripped off the tape and opened the cardboard box. Inside was a second box, labeled HANDLE WITH CARE. *EXTREME CARE*!

Chandler handed over his gardening gloves. He was accustomed to Mistery family surprises. Even so, his eyes nearly popped out of his head when Angela lifted out . . .

"A *cactus*?!" he blurted.

The girl's cheeks were flushed. "Not just any cactus!" she exclaimed, in seventh heaven. "A very rare specimen!"

It looked like a squat green gourd bristling with thorns. There was also a small birthday card with a picture of llamas.

Darling Agatha,

 Daddy and I are thrilled to have found you the last existing potted *Indionigro petrificus* in the world. You can plant it in Lot 42. Add a pinch of sand, don't overwater, and be sure to wear gardening gloves—the spines contain a dangerous, paralyzing toxin that causes apparent death (but just for a few hours!).

 Big hugs and kisses,

 Mom

"A paralyzing toxin! That *rocks*!" Agatha was overjoyed.

She said a hasty good-bye to the butler and ran to the greenhouse, cactus in hand.

The sun beat down on the structure, which looked like a giant Victorian birdhouse with its white wrought-iron frame and glass panels. Inside, it was stiflingly hot, at least twenty degrees warmer than the hot summer air outside. The air was still, with a fragrance of moondrops and century plant blossoms. Agatha looked around. There were cacti of every size and shape, some round as billiard balls, others tall and lean, their arms raised like gawky scarecrows.

It was a scene straight out of a Wild West movie.

Agatha squinted at the small metal numbers on the planting trays. "Lot 37 . . . Lot 38 . . . here it is, Lot 42!"

Next to a cluster of prickly pears was a bare square of sandy soil, ready for planting. Agatha carefully set down her *petrificus* and went to a nearby hutch for a trowel. On impulse, she also grabbed a guidebook on South American succulents and a second on poisons and antidotes.

You never could tell.

Chandler's gardening gloves were so huge it was hard to hold on to the trowel. Laughing, she tightened the elastic around both wrists, but they still looked like boxing gloves on her small hands.

Agatha stood stock-still for a moment, staring at the *petrificus* and starting to work out the plot of a book featuring an "apparent death." Maybe a murderer who staged his own funeral, then returned in secret to take revenge on somebody . . .

"Ahem," Chandler cleared his throat. Agatha spun around. For a huge man, his approach was

incredibly quiet. "There would seem to be a slight problem."

"A problem, Chandler? What sort of a problem?"

"It relates to young Dashiell, Miss."

"Dash?! What does he want?"

"I believe it would be best if you come take a look, Miss Agatha."

With a deep sigh, Agatha pulled off her gloves and followed him out of the greenhouse, stopping under a chestnut tree.

Perched on a branch was a homing pigeon, shuffling nervously. He had good reason.

Watson, Agatha's Siberian cat, was half hidden in the ferns, licking his whiskers.

"Watson! Come here!" Agatha called out.

The cat gave the pigeon a look that said, "Later for you, bud." Then he wound himself around Agatha's legs, purring.

Agatha wasn't impressed. She climbed up the

tree and grabbed hold of the pigeon. Untying the tin cylinder from its leg so Dash would know she'd received his message, she launched the bird into the air, where it flew away with a flurry of wings.

Inside the cylinder was a rolled piece of paper. Agatha was used to surprises, but this was a doozy:

AGENT DM14 DEPARTING FOR EGYPT 10:45, HEATHROW AIRPORT. TICKETS BOOKED. WILL SHARE DETAILS ON PLANE!

Still in the tree, Agatha looked at her watch. It was just after seven.

"Pack our bags, Chandler!" she shouted, "We're leaving immediately!"

Chandler didn't blink. "What sort of climate should we expect, Miss?"

Agatha thought for a split second. "Hot and

dry, like the greenhouse. Linen and cotton shirts, cargo shorts . . ."

"As you wish, Miss Agatha."

The butler disappeared into the Mistery Estate, trailed by a hungry Watson.

Agatha shimmied back down the tree trunk and followed them in, going straight to her room. On one wall was a giant family tree, a map of the world notated with the home address, occupation, and relationship of every known member of the Mistery family.

She put her finger on Egypt and found a distant aunt living in Luxor. "Patricia Mistery!" she exclaimed. "Camel breeder!"

Satisfied, she picked up the phone and told Aunt Patricia they were on their way.

Half an hour later, she and Chandler climbed into the limo. Agatha wore khakis and desert boots, and Chandler had on a Hawaiian shirt the

size of a pup tent. He carried two overstuffed suitcases. Agatha carried a gift box containing the toxic *petrificus* (it might come in handy) and Watson's carrier. As soon as the limo peeled out, she unlatched it, and the Siberian cat curled up on her lap.

They were off! There was only one problem: Would Dash be on time?

CHAPTER TWO

Destination Luxor

*A*gatha's parents were allergic to all normal methods of transportation. They liked parasails, hang gliders, and hot-air balloons for wafting around the English countryside, and when they went overseas, they preferred to travel by donkey cart, broken-down jeep, or vintage steamboat.

"We Misterys are adventurers!" her father would chuckle. "A jumbo jet? Ha! Doesn't have half the charm of an ocean liner like the *Titanic*!"

Agatha rolled her eyes. "Dad, the *Titanic* was sunk by an iceberg," she would remind him. He'd take a few puffs on his pipe and change the subject.

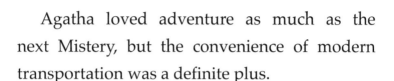

Agatha loved adventure as much as the next Mistery, but the convenience of modern transportation was a definite plus.

Especially when she was in a hurry.

The limo dodged through London traffic and sped to the airport. Agatha and Chandler found two tickets booked under their names at the VIP check-in desk. Within minutes, they boarded a luxurious Egyptair Boeing 777, nonstop to Luxor. Surrounded by cool air conditioning, they took their seats and placed Watson's carrier in the seat reserved for Dash.

The Siberian cat was used to flying and was already fast asleep. Agatha buried her nose in a book. She had brought the two volumes on cacti and poisons, along with some guidebooks on Egypt. She began with the book about poisons, looking for more information about her new *Indionigro petrificus*. Chandler shifted around,

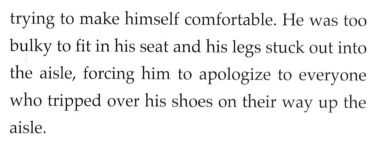

trying to make himself comfortable. He was too bulky to fit in his seat and his legs stuck out into the aisle, forcing him to apologize to everyone who tripped over his shoes on their way up the aisle.

They watched as Egyptians and tourists boarded in droves. There were families on summer vacations and young couples going on

honeymoons. Soon, the plane was full and the roar of the engines got louder with each passing minute.

"Flight attendants, prepare to depart," the captain said over the loudspeaker.

Chandler raised his eyebrows. "Where is Dash?" he asked, looking worried.

Agatha twisted around, peering back at the hatch. "He's arguing with a flight attendant," she sighed. "Typical!"

They pricked up their ears to listen in.

"I told you, it isn't a cell phone, so I don't need to turn it off during takeoff," Dash was telling a young flight attendant. "It's a new generation of Nintendo!"

"It's so small!" she said, frowning suspiciously. "Show me!"

With an impatient snort, Dash unhooked his titanium gadget from the strap of his bag, pressed a button, and handed it to her.

The attendant stared at the flashing screen and seemed to relax. "And it plays *Super Mario*, too?" she asked. "Where can I buy one?"

Dash scooped it out of her hand with impressive dexterity. "It's kind of a prototype model," he told her. "It isn't on sale yet."

"But . . . but . . ."

"So, I can go now, right?"

Without waiting for an answer, Dash strode down the aisle. The fake screen trick had worked perfectly. He felt like a real secret agent.

Agatha waved at him, but he was whistling happily, lost in fantasies of becoming the world's greatest spyware designer.

"Watch out!" warned his cousin.

"Huh, what?!"

Too late.

Dash didn't see Chandler's leg poking into the aisle. He tripped and fell onto the carpet, yelping in pain. Then he started frantically scrabbling

around on the floor, searching under the other passengers' seats.

"Where is it?!" he screeched. "I can't find it!"

Agatha tried to calm him. "Find what? Can I help?"

"My EyeNet! It's gone! So much for our mission."

So *that* was why he was freaking out.

The EyeNet was the state-of-the-art gadget the Eye International Detective Academy gave to its students. Dash never let his EyeNet out of his sight, and he felt lost without it.

"It fell into Watson's carrier," Chandler reassured him.

Dash lunged to retrieve it, forgetting one minor detail: the cat hated his guts.

Sure enough, as soon as he stuck his hand into the case, Watson recognized his scent and chomped down on his finger.

"Owww!" Dash groaned. But at least he'd retrieved his precious gadget, and that was the main thing he cared about. He sank into his seat with a sigh of relief.

"Tough life, this detective gig," Agatha deadpanned.

"You know it, cousin!"

Moments later, the plane taxied onto the

airstrip and angled up into the sky, piercing the pale London cloud cover. Above it, the sky was a peaceful, clear blue. Time to find out more about Dash's mission.

"Tell me everything, Agent DM14!" Agatha urged him.

"Oh yeah, right. I nearly forgot . . ."

"Come on, spill!"

Dash told her about the message he'd gotten from his school that morning. It was his final exam for Investigation Techniques: he had three days to find out who'd stolen an artifact from an archaeological dig in the Valley of the Kings. "It's some kind of tablet about some mysterious pharaoh," he added.

"Some kind of tablet? Could you be any less vague?"

"That's all I know, Agatha!"

"Are you sure?"

Dash ran his hands through his messy hair, looking embarrassed. "Well, I haven't checked out all the video files yet. I wanted to watch them with you . . ."

"So what are we waiting for?"

"Um, right. Here goes!"

Dash pulled all the gear out of his backpack: two sets of earbuds, an adapter, and a USB cable. He connected the various pieces to the EyeNet, then switched on the television screen on the back of the seat in front of him. He proudly switched on his device.

Onscreen, an older man with a basset-hound face and a mustache appeared, introducing himself as agent UM60. "That's my Investigation Tech teacher," said Dash.

"Luxor, the ancient capital of Egypt, was once known as Thebes," the teacher intoned. "It's renowned for its temples honoring the sun.

But you, agent DM14, must go to the opposite shore of the Nile, where the sun sets and the pharaohs have slept in their tombs for thousands of years: that endless necropolis known as the Valley of the Kings. I assume you're familiar with Tutankhamen's curse?"

Dash squirmed. Apparently not.

Agatha was hypnotized by the slide show of images on the screen. It was like a crash course in Egypt's archaeological wonders.

"Remember, this is an exam, not a vacation," the teacher warned. "You must discover the culprit within three days, agent DM14, or I will be forced to fail you!"

Dash jolted back in his seat, beads of sweat popping up on his forehead. Exams always made him incredibly nervous. That was why he always brought Agatha with him whenever he had to go out on a mission.

Meanwhile, Agent UM60 wrapped up his

speech: "Obviously you will have access to all of our data on Egypt, but the clues must be found in the field. Do I make myself clear?"

The video clip came to an end, and the professor's long face was replaced with an endless menu of files: satellite maps, coded messages, and footage from spy-cams.

"It's worse than I thought!" Dash moaned. "I'll never get through this!"

Agatha patted his shoulder. "Don't worry." She grinned. "Piece of cake. This is going to be fun!"

They pulled out their earbuds, and only then noticed that all the other passengers were staring at them, irritated.

The flight attendant who'd been so excited by the *Super Mario* game now looked angry. "Which one of you is Agent DM14?" she demanded, crossing her arms.

Absolute silence.

Dash shrank into his seat, dipping his chin so his hair flopped down over his eyes.

"I am," lied Chandler. "Is there a problem, ma'am?"

"Can't you see what a mess you've made?"

"What do you mean?"

"Your bizarre documentary is playing on every TV screen on this plane!"

"Really?"

"Our passengers have the right to watch whatever in-flight movie they choose, and I'll thank you not to take over the airwaves!"

There was a roar of agreement from the other passengers. A few even clapped.

Chandler didn't blink. "Whatever you say, ma'am. My sincerest apologies."

What a disaster.

As soon as the flight attendant took off, Agatha thanked Chandler for his quick thinking and

turned to her cousin. "Let's bag on the research till later, okay, Dash?" she said with a smile.

"Good plan," he agreed. "We'll check out the files in the shadow of the pyramids. Sounds pretty cool, right?"

Agatha looked at him, amused. "Very cool. Just one problem: there aren't any pyramids in Luxor or in the Valley of the Kings. Unless you mean the mountain peak of al-Qurn."

Dash scowled. "No pyramids?" he muttered under his breath. "Some detective I am!"

Queen of the Lemons

*N*ot in her wildest dreams could Agatha have imagined the splendors of Luxor. The airport was brand-new, and its vast plate-glass windows looked out over a colorful city that seemed to vibrate with life.

Even Dash, who'd been snoring for four hours straight, rubbed his eyes in amazement.

"Awesome!" He stopped to exclaim every couple of steps. "Did you see that jackal-headed statue? And check out that giant sphinx!"

"Dash, they're just copies," Agatha said. "The real statues are inside the Temple of Luxor and in Karnak."

"How do you know?" Dash frowned.

"I read up on them while you were sleeping."

He spun around in alarm. "You didn't use my EyeNet, did you?"

Agatha held up a guidebook. "No, Dash. Sometimes you can find answers in things without screens."

Tailed by a silent Chandler, who was dragging the two biggest suitcases, they passed through the automatic glass doors and into an ocean of people.

The hot air hit them like a blast from a furnace. If London was having a summer heat wave, it was nothing compared to midday in Luxor. The square was a jumble of palm trees and souvenir stands selling postcards, beads, and embroidered robes. Taxi drivers blared their horns happily, and the spicy smells of roasting kebabs wafted through the still air.

Through the riot of color and chaotic voices

shouting in various languages, Agatha thought she heard somebody call out her name.

"Did you hear that, too?" she asked.

Before Dash and Chandler could answer, she heard a loud, "AGATHA! YOO-HOO!"

In the center of the square, under an ancient stone obelisk, was a squadron of camels that would have made Lawrence of Arabia jealous. Sitting upright on a carved wooden saddle surrounded by blankets and fringe, a plump, forty-year-old woman in orange embroidered pajamas and a straw hat was waving her hand.

Agatha knew right away who it must be: Aunt Patricia!

"Yoo-hoo, Auntie! We're here!" she called, making a megaphone with her hands.

Patricia Mistery's eyes gleamed with joy. She dismounted in no time and pushed her way through the crowd, charging forward with open arms.

"My dear children!" she said, misty-eyed. "At long last we meet in person! I'm a great friend of both your dads, Arthur and Edgar!"

She gave Agatha a giant hug, planting a loud smacking kiss on her cheek. Then she moved on to Chandler with open arms.

"Ah . . . I'm just the butler," he stammered, embarrassed.

Aunt Patricia took a step backward, assessing his size. "Actually I did think you were a bit . . . mature to be Edgar's son." Her attention shifted to the teenage boy hiding behind the ex-heavyweight. "So you are young Dashiell?"

"Yes, ma'am," Dash replied, shrinking back from her hug.

Aunt Patricia burst out laughing and ruffled his hair. "Are you a shy boy? Too bad. You must break all the girls' hearts!"

Dash blushed as red as a tomato.

"I hope you're all hungry and haven't been

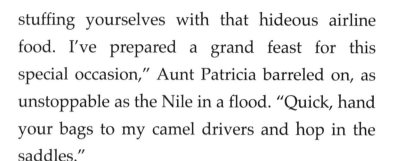

stuffing yourselves with that hideous airline food. I've prepared a grand feast for this special occasion," Aunt Patricia barreled on, as unstoppable as the Nile in a flood. "Quick, hand your bags to my camel drivers and hop in the saddles."

Agatha nodded and catapulted herself onto the back of a camel. It was a little like sitting on top of a draft horse, if the horse had a grain bag stuffed under its saddle. Dash and Chandler had a harder time mounting their camels. Dash's camel snorted and spat at him. "None of that, Nero!" Aunt Patricia said sternly, and the camel obeyed. Chandler's camel sagged under his weight as if he were a slab of stone.

The caravan wound its way slowly through the city traffic, setting off colorful protests from people in cars. They turned onto an avenue lined with palm trees and stopped in front of an

imposing gate decorated with hieroglyphs.

They had arrived at Patricia Mistery's sumptuous villa.

Inside the courtyard, the children refreshed themselves with water from a splashing fountain and followed their aunt into the dining room, which looked like a royal tent for Cleopatra. The floor was covered with rich carpets and silken cushions. A sweet smell of incense wafted through the air.

Watson wandered about, curiously sniffing a sculpture of a cat goddess, losing interest when he realized it smelled of old rock, not of cat.

"Later today I'll take you to see the Temple of Luxor," said Patricia, popping an almond-stuffed date in her mouth. "And tomorrow we'll head out to Karnak. Does that sound like fun?"

Dash swallowed a mouthful of couscous the wrong way and started to cough.

"Auntie, we're terribly sorry." Agatha came to his rescue. "Dash and I need to leave right away for the Valley of the Kings."

"Well, I was planning to take you there right after Luxor, but we can do it in whatever order you like!"

Dash took a long sip of water, thumping himself on the chest.

"So sorry, but we need to go by ourselves," said Agatha. "I mean, just the two of us—plus Chandler and Watson, of course."

Patricia realized something was up. "Aha! An adventure in the usual Mistery style." She

beamed. "Tell me, what's your destination?"

"Tomb 66," Dash said, suddenly remembering a detail from his EyeNet.

"What?!" Patricia jumped up in astonishment. "Tomb 66 has never been found!"

Agatha gave Dash a poke in the ribs. "You didn't mention that little detail," she muttered. "You said you'd tell me everything!"

"Um, yeah, it was in one of the files I downloaded in London."

Patricia clapped her hands to summon a servant. He brought in a map of the Valley of the Kings, rolling it out like a magic carpet in the

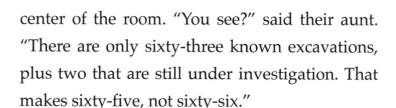

center of the room. "You see?" said their aunt. "There are only sixty-three known excavations, plus two that are still under investigation. That makes sixty-five, not sixty-six."

"Can I turn the TV on?" asked Dash, edging away.

"Be my guest," she replied, showing Agatha and Chandler the chart of tomb excavations.

Meanwhile, Dash hooked up his EyeNet and started playing a black-and-white film clip, cranking the volume up with the remote.

Everyone turned around, even Watson.

"We don't know exactly to whom Tomb 66 belonged," wheezed a white-bearded Egyptologist with a French accent. "But we speculate it was a pharaoh of the New Kingdom who was disgraced and never recorded in the royal records. This could be a revolutionary discovery, but without the stolen tablet our hands are tied. We must get it back, *tout de suite*!"

The camera cut to a shot of the sandy route leading to Tomb 66. It wound behind the temple district and climbed high up into the hills.

"So that's my mission!" exclaimed Dash. "Now I get it!"

Aunt Patricia looked puzzled. "A mission?" she said. "What do you mean by that?"

Agatha felt obliged to explain. "Dash is a student at Eye Academy, the famous detective school and investigative agency. We're on a mission to help him pass an exam."

Patricia didn't need to hear another word. She called a dozen servants, who all came running. "Prepare some provisions and saddle three camels instantly! Book them a barge! And dig up some video cameras and microphones!" she rattled off.

"Video cameras and microphones, Auntie?" Agatha asked. "What for?"

Patricia leaned on a column. "The Egyptian

Supreme Council of Antiquities won't let just anyone wander around in the Valley of the Kings," she explained. "The permits are highly restrictive, and there are guards everywhere!"

"But where do the video cameras come in?"

"You could pretend to be a BBC film crew, making a documentary on ancient Egypt." She paused for a moment. "What do you think?"

Agatha was impressed with this ingenious plan. "Great idea, Auntie!" she said. "All right, let's take a look at you!"

Dash and Chandler stood at attention.

"All right, Dash can be the cinematographer," Agatha said decidedly. "Chandler, you'll play the part of the wealthy producer."

"And what about you?"

"Microphone, notebook, and pen: I'll be the reporter," she said, grinning.

Patricia Mistery clapped appreciatively. "That's the spirit!"

It took them more than an hour to find the equipment and load up the camels. Dash took advantage of the downtime to print out some key documents, handing them to his cousin for safekeeping. He still wasn't comfortable riding a camel, and he was afraid he might lose precious data if he fell off.

Next, they all went into guest bedrooms to change their clothes. When they came back out, they looked exactly like a professional television crew.

"Perfect!" Patricia exclaimed, handing out press passes. "Now I'll accompany you to the boat I've booked, so you can cross the Nile!"

But as soon as they got to the courtyard, a nasty surprise met their eyes: Hasan, one of the camel handlers in their aunt's service, sat on the edge of the fountain, stiff as a statue.

His colleagues were muttering, frightened. Nobody dared to touch him.

"What happened?" demanded Patricia Mistery.

"It's a curse," they responded in chorus. "The punishment of the serpent Apep!"

Agatha had already guessed what had happened. Inspecting Hasan's hands, she discovered a needlelike spine stuck in his palm.

"*Indionigro petrificus*," she whispered to herself. "Hasan must have touched the cactus while he was loading it into the saddlebags!"

Luckily she had just finished reading the book on poisons and knew an antidote to the paralyzing toxin. "Auntie, have you got a couple of lemons?" she asked.

In a flash, Patricia darted into the kitchen and came back with a basket of lemons.

Agatha squeezed a few drops of juice onto Hasan's dry lips, then used the peel to remove the spine.

Like magic, the handler came back to life and

stretched. "What happened?" he asked, looking dazed.

His colleagues cheered, waving their arms in the air and singing a song in Agatha's honor.

"What are they saying, Auntie?"

Patricia Mistery smiled, pleased. "That you have the power to waken the dead. They believe you're the reincarnation of Isis, queen of the underworld!"

"Queen of the underworld?" Dash said with a snort. "More like queen of the lemons!"

Under Surveillance

"Aunt Patricia is kind of . . . eccentric," said Dash, leaning over the railing to stare at the muddy waters of the Nile. Was that a log floating ahead or a crocodile?

"Big surprise," countered Agatha. "She's a Mistery, right? Our whole family's got a few screws loose."

"Yeah, sure . . . but where did she come up with this tugboat? What do you think?"

"Stinky, rusty, and slow. My parents would love it."

They both laughed, watching the old tugboat's

funnel belch clouds of black smoke. Two long-masted boats with graceful, triangular sails—*feluccas*, thought Agatha happily—glided past them.

Before she said good-bye, Aunt Patricia had assured them. "The *Duat* won't attract attention from anyone. I've instructed the crew to dock at an abandoned pier near the foot of the path on your map. Will this suit you, dear children?"

At the sound of "abandoned pier," Dash gave a weak smile.

But Agatha was more excited than ever. Thumbing through her dictionary of ancient Egyptian, she informed everyone that the name "Duat" meant "afterlife." This news depressed Dash even more.

The afterlife tug was no speedboat, but at least it would get them where they had to go. To the abandoned pier. Dash gulped as the dark shape ahead took a sudden dive, flashing its scaly tail. *Not* a log.

"I propose we look over those downloads," said Agatha, popping open her travel umbrella for shade. "Okay with you, cousin?"

Dash nodded, glad to think about anything besides crocodiles.

They made themselves comfortable upwind of the camels' enclosure and pored over the printouts.

Meanwhile, Chandler was busy chasing Watson around the deck. Quick as lightning, the cat scurried between sailors' legs, hiding in the most unlikely places.

"Okay, here's a file on that Egyptologist from the film clip," said Agatha.

"Professor Maigret, right?"

"Hercule Maigret of the Sorbonne."

"The Sore Bun?" Dash echoed.

She raised her eyebrows. "The Sorbonne? World-famous university in Paris?" Sometimes Agatha wondered if Dash ever studied. "The file says he has two assistants, one Polish and one German, and twenty-one Egyptian laborers," she continued, licking her finger to flick through the pages.

Suddenly she spotted a curious photograph. She pulled it out.

It was a full-length snapshot of four people, looking proud and satisfied. At their feet lay

an ancient clay tablet covered in tiny, chiseled hieroglyphs.

Dash peered at the photo. "Professor Maigret is the guy in the middle. You can tell by the Santa Claus beard," he laughed. "What are the other two names again?"

"Let me see . . ." Agatha pulled back a wisp of hair. "There's Dr. Paretsky, he's Polish and an expert in hieroglyphic writing, and Dr. Dortmunder from Germany, he's a geochemist."

"I bet Paretsky is the blond guy, and the chubby one is Dortmunder."

"Me too. But who is the fourth man?" she asked, almost talking to herself.

The man's tunic was decorated with glyphs, and his long, pointy beard gave him a sinister look. He had the air of an ancient Egyptian priest: someone who might turn you into a mummy.

"Wow, what hypnotic eyes!" Dash said with a shudder.

Meanwhile, Agatha flipped through the pages looking for any hint of his identity. "I'm afraid we won't know who he is until we get to Tomb 66," she said, disappointed. She drew a large question mark in her notebook and wrote underneath it: FOURTH MAN. "Can you bring that photo back up on your EyeNet?"

Dash nodded, his thumbs flying over the keypad. "Got it," he said.

"Good. Now zoom in on the tablet."

He did.

"Notice anything?"

"It looks thin and fragile, like pastry crust," Dash observed. "How could someone steal it without it crumbling to bits?"

"Excellent analysis, cousin!"

Agatha wrote down *TRANSPORTATION OF TABLET?* in her notebook. "Anything else?" she asked.

"Umm, don't think so . . ."

"Look harder, Dash."

He zoomed in even closer. He rubbed his chin and narrowed his eyes. "Is it something about the hieroglyphs?" he murmured doubtfully.

"Way to go, Dash! I pulled open one of the little drawers in my memory, and realized . . ." Agatha paused for dramatic effect.

Dash hung on her words: his cousin's prodigious photographic memory was legendary in the Mistery family.

"In the hieroglyphs compendium I studied last spring . . . ," she said, squinting at the screen. "Yes, I'm quite sure."

"Sure of what?"

"Don't quote me on this, but I think every hieroglyph on that tablet is carved in reverse!"

Reaching into her saddlebag, Agatha pulled out a makeup case.

Dash's jaw dropped. "So that means you're putting on lip gloss?"

"Don't be silly," Agatha winked. "A woman's purse is a useful tool kit. Check it out!"

She popped open a mirrored compact and set it in front of the screen.

In the mirror image, each hieroglyph seemed to be written the right way.

"Remember, they only had simple bronze mirrors back then, and no zoom key," said Agatha, resting her chin on her intertwined fingers. "Whoever carved these hieroglyphs

wanted to make sure they were a challenge to read."

Dash jumped to his feet, excited. "Of course!" he said. "That explains why Professor Maigret sounded so vague in the film . . ."

"He never had time to translate the tablet!" Agatha said, finishing his thought. She scrawled HIEROGLYPHS REVERSED in her notebook.

"What else?" she pressed.

But just at that moment, the *Duat*'s crew all started talking at once as the engine shut down with a groan and a shrill, metallic squawk. "Is it broken?" cried Dash.

He and Agatha were joined by Chandler, who had Watson tucked under one arm. "Looks like some trouble, Miss Agatha," he said.

"What's the matter?"

"It seems to be a police checkpoint."

A patrol boat sped toward them, water

spraying from the propeller. Then it pulled up alongside with machine guns pointing at the *Duat*.

Dash went as white as a sheet. "Aunt Patricia promised we wouldn't get any attention!" he screeched. "I call this a *lot* of attention!"

"Well, yelling won't help," said Agatha. "And we're not doing anything wrong."

"Right. Just pretending to be a TV crew to get to a tomb that's not opened yet. No problem there."

Agatha shushed him. In the tense moments that followed, a uniformed officer boarded the *Duat* with one hand on his gun belt. The captain came out of the cabin and met him on deck. The tugboat captain looked tough, with a grizzled face, hooked nose, and no-nonsense manner. He sent the crew away with a snap of his fingers, speaking quietly with the imposing policeman.

"I wish I spoke better Arabic," Agatha whispered.

"I wish I spoke *any*," said Dash. "Or maybe it's best not to know."

The policeman checked the tugboat's registration, took a quick glance at the cargo, including the camels, then pointed at Agatha and her companions.

"Where did we put those press passes?" muttered Dash. "Without them, our cover is blown!"

The captain continued to speak in low tones, then beckoned to them with an eloquent wave of his hand.

"We're done for!" Dash panicked. "They're going to arrest us!"

Agatha grabbed him by the front of his shirt. "Get a grip, Dash! Man up!"

She had to forcefully haul him in front of

the policeman, who greeted them with a toothy smile.

"He wants to be filmed by the BBC," the captain explained. "Do what he asks and keep your mouths shut. He doesn't speak very much English."

"Um, great. Good to know," said Dash awkwardly. He picked up his video camera and said, "Action! I think." Raising her microphone, Agatha signaled to the policeman, who furrowed his brow and moved through a series of Hollywood action-star poses.

"Bond, James Bond." He grinned, flashing two thumbs-up. "Shaken, no stir, yes?" He bounded dramatically back onto the patrol boat, which raced away, roaring.

The tugboat captain eyed Dash. "The police were looking for a gang of smugglers. That's not you three, is it?"

"Absolutely not!" Dash said with a gulp.

"Good," rasped the captain. "Next time, remember to take off the lens cap." Pulling down the brim of his cap, he strode back to the cabin.

Dash hit himself in the forehead. "Lens cap. Duh!" While he put the camera back into its case, Agatha filled Chandler in on their findings. He listened attentively, turning the photos in his giant hands.

Finally, late in the afternoon, they reached their destination.

The *Duat* had already chugged past great temples and riverside villages, heading for the barren hills to the north. The clusters of palm trees and farmland gave way to rougher terrain. Finally they docked at a rotting wooden pier, covered with wild vegetation.

Clearly no one had used it for years.

The three adventurers (plus camels and cat) quickly disembarked and found themselves on a scrub-covered plain, crisscrossed by muddy streams.

"I thought Egypt was all sand dunes and desert," said Dash, a little confused.

"The desert begins after you pass the mountains," Agatha told him. "Here, on the banks of the Nile, the land is fertile, especially during the summer flood season."

"How do you know that?" Dash demanded. "Wait, don't tell me. Because you're the rebooted queen of the underworld."

"Cut it out," she laughed. "All I did was memorize a few maps of this region."

"You and your famous memory drawers!" Dash said with a snort. "All right, open one up. Where's the trail? I can't get a GPS read on my EyeNet; no signal."

Agatha craned her neck, scanning the marshland. "It all looks like mud to me," she had to admit.

Chandler, who was twice her height and had better eyesight, pointed at a sloping hill in the distance.

"Dirt path up that hillside, Miss," he said quietly.

"Excellent, Chandler." Agatha smiled. "That must be where we need to go."

"Are you sure, cousin?" Dash asked.

She didn't respond: she was already clambering onto her camel with the skill of a born rider. Dash moaned, eyeing his camel. "No spitting this time, okay, dude?" Somehow he and Chandler got onto their camels in one piece. Agatha was already riding ahead, urging her camel forward as fast as it would go. Dash and Chandler struggled to catch up.

They rode through the back country for a good half hour and then took a dirt path that wound upward between the jagged peaks fringing the Valley of the Kings.

Agatha had to stop every few minutes to wait for her saddle-sore friends, and each time she took the chance to survey the landscape with a small pair of high-powered binoculars.

The path was rocky and steep, full of dangerous turns and unmarked intersections.

"The bad news is we could get lost," said Agatha, tapping her nose.

"And the good news?" Dash panted behind her.

Agatha put the binoculars back in the pocket of her khaki shirt. "No guards to get in our way," she said, getting back on the path.

But she was wrong.

Big-time.

Just before sunset, they stopped in a narrow gulch to recheck their coordinates. Suddenly they heard echoing noises. Raising their heads from the map, they saw gun barrels poking out from between the rocks.

"Don't move!" a man shouted in English.

At the sound of his bass voice, Dash started to shake. "This is serious business," he mumbled in terror. "This time we're really in trouble!"

Tomb 66

A dozen men swarmed into the gulch. They were armed, but no one was wearing a police or military uniform.

Who were they? Smugglers? Or tomb robbers?

"I have a very bad feeling about this," Agatha whispered. "Let's just stay calm and find out what they want."

Dash and Chandler nodded in silence.

In the dim glow of dusk, a flashlight beam cut through the air like a blade. When the light hit Dash, he jerked on his camel's reins and raised both arms high in the air. "We're innocent!" he cried. "We surrender!"

His sudden movement spooked his camel, which kicked and bucked, trying to shake off its saddle and rider.

The attackers watched as Dash twisted around, frantically trying to free his legs from the saddlebags, and they burst out laughing.

"Oh, this is just perfect!" groaned Dash. "I get to be mocked while I die!"

The rippling laughter was interrupted by a

French-accented voice: "You there! Give the boy some assistance!"

The sentence was uttered by a wiry, bald man with a white beard. It was Professor Maigret, the Egyptologist from the film clip.

Agatha dismounted and stepped forward to join him. "We're here about the stolen tablet, Professor," she informed him.

He looked momentarily startled. "What did you say?" he asked anxiously. "Is agent DM14 here?"

Agatha pointed at Chandler.

"At your service," the butler said, giving Agatha a knowing nod and clambering down from his camel.

Still flailing around in the saddlebag straps, Dash protested, "What? Um, no, there must be a mistake! This is my mission." But Professor Maigret was already shaking Chandler's huge hand.

"I'm happy you're here, Agent DM14," the scholar said, relieved. "Please pardon my crew for the unfriendly reception. There have been many strange things going on in these parts."

"You don't say," Chandler said stiffly.

"By the way, this is my hieroglyphs specialist, Doc—"

"A pleasure to meet you, Dr. Paretsky," Chandler said, recognizing the young scholar from the photograph. In real life, he appeared even paler, his thin shoulders hunched, his eyes watery.

"The pleasure is mine," the scholar replied in a low voice, intimidated by the butler's bulk.

Then he looked at Agatha and Dash. "But who are these children?" he asked, perplexed.

"Even master detectives need clever assistants," Chandler said gravely.

"*C'est vrai*, this is true," interjected Maigret, happily rubbing his hands together. Then he

turned to a handful of aides. "You will please escort our guests to base camp," he ordered.

As the group began to move, Dash sidled up behind Agatha, protesting. "I don't get it. *I'm* the master detective!"

"Lower your voice, please," Agatha said in a hushed tone.

"Tell me why you lied to them," Dash insisted.

"Simple," she said. "If they're focused on Chandler, we can move around more freely."

Dash thought about this for a moment, turning his gaze upward to the first stars of the night. "That makes sense," he admitted grudgingly. "Keep their eyes off us . . ."

"Let's run a quick check," Agatha suggested.

"A quick check of what?"

"Can your EyeNet detect heat sources?"

"Yes, of course. Why?"

"Activate the scanner when we get to base camp," she said. "According to our information,

there should be three scholars and twenty-one laborers, plus the fourth man from the photo, for a total of twenty-five people . . ."

Dash pulled out the EyeNet and punched in a sequence of keys. "Got it. You want to find out whether anyone's missing," he whispered.

"If the tablet was taken somewhere outside the main camp, the thieves will be with it as well. Am I right?" Agatha smiled and Dash nodded, impressed.

It was practically dark by the time they reached their destination, descending a long, sandy hill into base camp. Now that the sun had gone down, the desert air quickly grew cooler, and Agatha shivered.

They found themselves in a funnel-shaped valley surrounded by cliffs. In the silvery moonlight, the laborers' tents looked like floating ghosts.

Professor Maigret led his guests into the pavilion reserved for the heads of the expedition.

Just outside the kitchen, they came across the third Egyptologist, a rotund young German with his mouth smeared with chocolate ice cream.

"Nice to meet you, Dr. Dortmunder." Chandler spoke without hesitation, easing into the role of a master detective.

The geologist appeared stunned to be recognized. He quickly swallowed the last of his chocolate-cherry ice-cream pop. "Is anyone hungry?" he mumbled with his mouth full. "I was just having a predinner snack . . ."

While the two assistants cleared the table of papers and tools, Maigret took the butler's arm, planning to show the lab tent to the master detective.

Agatha drew close to her cousin's ear. "What's the head count?" she whispered.

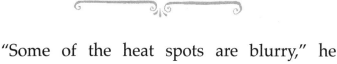

"Some of the heat spots are blurry," he murmured. "I count twenty-three. Looks like there are two people missing!"

"Interesting. Extremely interesting." Agatha nodded.

Soon after, the pavilion filled with the smell of sizzling sausage and crispy potatoes, served on tin plates. It was a far cry from Aunt Patricia's exotic feast, but it was hearty and filling.

Everyone wolfed down their food in silence, even Maigret and Chandler. The bony Paretsky pushed his potatoes aside, but Dr. Dortmunder ate seconds and thirds. Watson sat in Agatha's lap and, with a swipe of his paw, stole a whole sausage right off Dash's plate.

He didn't even notice.

Agatha decided to break the ice. "When you found us, were you searching for the two laborers who disappeared?" she asked casually.

The scholars looked at each other, astonished.

"How do you know about that?" asked Maigret, nervously wiping his mouth. "We haven't told anyone outside the camp!"

"It's our job," Chandler said drily. "We're here to investigate."

The oldest Egyptologist was delighted. "What did I tell you?" he told his assistants. "The Eye International detectives are the best in the world! See, they're already on top of this mystery!" Then he turned to Chandler. "Where would you like to begin, *monsieur*?"

"At the beginning, of course."

By the light of the halogen lamps, Professor Maigret began to recount the sequence of events from the time they first left for the Valley of the Kings, about a month earlier.

Maigret and his assistants had followed the lead on an ancient piece of papyrus, preserved in the Museum of Egyptian Antiquities in Cairo,

which spoke of a cursed pharaoh. His tomb, numbered sixty-six by the Egyptian experts, appeared to be somewhere deep in the funnel-shaped valley. They had begun excavating immediately: days and days under the burning sun without even finding a coconut shell. Until finally Jafar, the director of operations, let out an exultant shout.

They all rushed to see what he'd unearthed and found themselves staring openmouthed at a large, clay tablet.

"Jafar," Agatha murmured to herself. "That's the name of the fourth man!"

She wanted to tell Dash right away, but just at that moment Dr. Dortmunder started to speak, describing the techniques they'd used to recover the relic. Because the ancient clay was so fragile, extracting the tablet had required surgical precision. It had been brought

to the lab for analysis less than a week ago.

"We knew at once what a sensational find it was," Dr. Paretsky broke in. "I swear, in my whole career, I've never seen anything like it!"

"Doctor, are you referring to the backward hieroglyphs?" Agatha asked.

Once again, the three scholars' dumbstruck expressions proved her right.

"Yes, the hieroglyphs," he said gloomily. "When we finished cleaning the tablet that night, I deciphered the first few sentences . . ."

"What did it say?" Chandler asked.

"They described a magnificent tomb that priests had secretly moved to this valley after an uprising," he said. "Unfortunately I didn't have time to find out its location before . . ."

"You see, we were in desperate need of sleep," Professor Maigret went on. "So we decided to continue our study the following morning."

"But by morning, the tablet was gone," finished Agatha.

"And two laborers . . . poof . . . vanished into thin air," Dash added.

Paretsky's face reddened. "You mean those despicable thieves?" he said, banging his fist on the plank table. "They stole our treasure from under our noses while we were asleep. You know nothing about it, boy!"

Dash frowned, offended. Dr. Dortmunder grabbed another ice-cream pop from the freezer and unwrapped it. The tension was palpable.

"Don't jump to conclusions, Dr. Paretsky," Chandler said calmly. "The investigation has just begun."

Agatha confirmed this with a nod. "Did anyone see the men leave?" she asked.

Maigret began to pace around the table. "That night, Jafar and two of his workers were on guard

duty," he recounted. "We questioned them all, but they insist that no one passed the checkpoint."

"I bet they climbed right up the cliffs," Dr. Paretsky snarled again. "I swear, if I ever get my hands on those miserable—"

"Well, that's all we know about the situation," Professor Maigret concluded hurriedly. "What else can we do to help you?"

Agatha drummed her fingers on the bridge of her nose, as she always did when her imagination started spinning.

After a few seconds, she smiled.

"First, we'll need to consult with the detective in private," she said. "If you don't mind, we'll all be back soon to tell you exactly how we intend to proceed."

The scholars had no choice but to agree.

Cultivating an air of professional cool, the three detectives got up from the table and walked outside into the night.

The Pharaoh's Curse

$\mathcal{A}$s soon as they left the pavilion, Agatha started to pace back and forth, thinking hard, her chin tucked down low.

"Something's not adding up," she said to herself. "I'm not sure what it is yet, but a good walk would help clear my head," she concluded, looking up. "I propose we take a look at the excavation site."

Dash and Chandler followed a few paces behind her, lighting the way with flashlights. They passed a supply shed with a military jeep parked behind it and finally came to the quarry

where the tablet had been found. It was cordoned off with barbed-wire fencing and a sign stating AUTHORIZED PERSONNEL ONLY. They walked right up to the base of the cliffs. A bare stretch of rocky terrain led to the only entrance into the valley.

The entrance was guarded by a small group of laborers armed with rifles.

Within twenty minutes, the trio had made a complete circuit of the valley's perimeter, but Agatha wasn't satisfied. She scrambled up onto a large, flat rock, surveying the moonlit cliffs.

Chandler and Dash could tell that her brain was working at top speed. They waited.

"There's only one possibility!" she exclaimed suddenly.

"What?" asked Dash.

Agatha jumped off the boulder. "Two things," she began. "First of all, it's clear that two laborers left in a rush without passing the checkpoint. That

makes them highly suspicious," she concluded. "Secondly . . ."

"Secondly?" Dash echoed, hanging on every word.

"They must have had an accomplice," she said, bending to pet Watson.

"An accomplice?!" marveled the young detective, tousling his hair with his hand. "What makes you think so?"

"Let's start with the motive, Dash," Agatha explained. "Let's say these two workers have stolen the tablet. What would they do with it?"

"I don't know," he stammered. "Maybe sell it to a collector or on the black market?"

"It's not a gold necklace," said Agatha. "It's a crumbling piece of old clay. Only an expert would know its true value."

Dash sat on a rock. "Good point. Why steal a lump of clay covered in code? It's an interesting

artifact, but its only real use would be finding the tomb . . ."

"Exactly." Agatha glowed. "And the thief must be someone who knows how fragile the tablet is. If the workers climbed up those steep cliffs with it, they must have taken great care not to break it. Someone with experience transporting fragile antiquities must have told them how to do it," she finished. "So our list of suspects is reduced to four: Jafar and his Egyptologist friends, obviously!"

"The scientists? But . . . but . . . they called us in!" Dash protested. "How could they be accomplices?"

"All four are experts in their fields, and each of them has a good reason to keep the tablet for himself." Agatha paused to observe her companions.

Her lanky cousin was stirring his hair into

tangles. Chandler rubbed his square jaw.

"I think I get it," said Dash. "Whoever's the first to uncover the cursed pharaoh's tomb will get all the fame and glory!"

Chandler nodded. "What is the game plan, Miss Agatha?" he asked.

Glancing over her shoulder to make sure that no one was listening, she said, "The best thing to do is to separate the suspects into two groups, Jafar in one, scientists in the other. They'll need to be kept busy while we search for evidence that will lead straight to our accomplice."

Dash and Chandler agreed that it sounded like a good plan.

There was only one problem.

"How are we going to separate them and keep them busy?"

"We'll come up with something," said Agatha. "In fact, I've already got an idea . . ."

The three of them brainstormed for several more minutes while Dash looked up satellite maps on his EyeNet.

The plan they came up with was risky, but they would just have to play their roles convincingly and take control of the situation.

With a nod of agreement, they stepped back onto the hard-packed path between tents. The laborers snored like a discordant orchestra.

Dr. Dortmunder spotted them first. "They're coming back," he announced to his colleagues in the kitchen.

They all took their seats around the table. In formal tones, Agatha started the speech they had planned. "Thanks to our infrared satellite images, Agent DM14 has located the two fugitives at the Abu Sidan oasis, fifty kilometers due east, in the desert." Not one word of this was the truth, but she made it sound absolutely convincing. This was another of Agatha's talents.

"As soon as the sun comes up, we'll take the jeep and some rifles," continued Chandler, playing his part perfectly. "We will catch the thieves by surprise and return with the tablet by nightfall."

The scholars cried out in delight. They shook Chandler's hand, patting the master detective's shoulder. Dr. Paretsky hung back a bit, still intimidated by his bulk.

"That means we can get back to work at the dig," rejoiced Professor Maigret, suddenly filled with the energy of a twenty-year-old. "Maybe

we'll finally discover the cursed pharaoh's tomb!"

But his joy disappeared when Agatha shook her head. "Professor, sir," she explained politely. "Agent DM14 will need your support on his mission. All three of you."

"What?!" hissed Dr. Paretsky. "Why us?"

"You know the two laborers and speak their language," Agatha explained.

Chandler's stubbly jaw tightened as he loomed over the table. "Would you prefer to risk the thieves escaping and taking the tablet with them?" he boomed, leaving no room for argument.

The three scholars immediately stopped complaining.

"Great, now that that's settled, we can move on," said Dash. "Where are we sleeping tonight? We're completely exhausted." He leaned on the freezer, yawning repeatedly. Like Agatha, he was

completely convincing: his role had been very well cast.

Agatha seized her chance. "Why don't we stay in the missing laborers' tent?" she suggested to Maigret. This would give them the perfect chance to start investigating immediately. "Unless someone else has moved into it?"

"No, no, it's still empty," he said, hesitating. "But we turned it upside down, searching. It's a mess!"

"No problem." Agatha winked at Dash, whose bedroom was always a pigsty. "I'm sure we've seen worse."

"Well then, Dr. Dortmunder will escort you there," replied the professor, looking at Chandler. "Does breakfast at seven suit your schedule, sir?"

Agatha took Dash by the arm. "Better make it seven thirty. This guy is a world-class sleeper," she joked.

Everyone said good night.

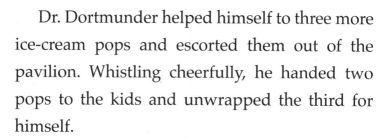

Dr. Dortmunder helped himself to three more ice-cream pops and escorted them out of the pavilion. Whistling cheerfully, he handed two pops to the kids and unwrapped the third for himself.

Chandler walked behind them in silence, toting the saddlebags and a folding chair he had brought from the kitchen.

Between bites of ice cream, Dr. Dortmunder showered Agatha with compliments. "Such remarkable insight! Mm, aren't these yummy? Brilliant detective work. How did you manage to track down the thieves so quickly?"

"We've got a great teacher," she shrugged, glancing at the trusty butler.

"You're so modest, Miss!"

The scholar chuckled, rubbing the round belly that spilled out from under his T-shirt. Then he stopped in front of a lopsided tent and unzipped

the mosquito net guarding the entrance. "Here's your royal palace," he said. "If you need water, the tank is down that way. Sweet dreams to all!"

Before joining her companions, Agatha watched him waddle down the path, whistling.

"He's gone," she whispered, pulling back the tent flap.

Dash was already out like a light, snoring on one of the cots, while Chandler had settled himself into the folding chair. He had gotten used to sleeping sitting up when he had worked the night shift at a hotel desk.

"What are you doing, you slackers?" Agatha scolded them. "I asked to stay in this tent so we could search for clues, not go to sleep!"

Chandler opened his eyes and sprang to his feet. "Certainly, Miss Agatha," he said quickly.

Dash didn't budge. "Can't it wait till tomorrow?" he droned in a hollow voice.

"No, Dash."

Eyelids drooping, Dash dragged himself up from the cot and attempted to stand. His body sagged like a mummy. "Sorry, verticality issues," he mumbled, sliding down onto a pile of clothes left behind by the laborers.

A split second later, he was asleep again.

"Guess it's just us, Chandler," Agatha sighed.

He nodded and hung up a battery-powered lantern, flooding the tent with light.

They started to poke through the mess. Chandler lifted a bath towel, uncovering a stash of Egyptian goods: cups, small pots, ashtrays, and coasters decorated with pictures of pharaohs and gods.

"Very curious," he observed.

Agatha turned a bust over and started to laugh. The label read MADE IN CHINA.

"It looks like our two laborers sold souvenirs

on the side," she said, tapping the bridge of her nose. "Which makes me think they were . . ."

"What, Miss Agatha?"

But she didn't have time to respond.

"ARGHHH!" yelled Dash. "That stupid cat!"

Watson ran over to Agatha. "What happened?" she asked.

"That furry monster was licking my ear," screeched Dash. "Feel this . . . it's all slimy!"

He lowered his voice. "Why are you staring at me like that?"

Agatha strode over and peeled off a piece of paper that had stuck to his cheek.

There was a message written on it, composed in Arabic letters cut out of a newspaper.

"Instant Translate," said Agatha. Dash was already scanning it onto his EyeNet.

"It says . . . pathetic *fellah*." He looked at his cousin. "*Fellah*?"

"*Fellahin* are Egyptian peasants. Go on."

Dash read: "You will be struck by the pharaoh's curse if you do not leave by dawn!"

Agatha's heart beat faster.

"This changes everything!" she gushed. "The tablet is still here! Nobody stole it! It's right in this camp!"

CHAPTER SEVEN
Everything's Backward in Egypt

The next morning, the three detectives awoke bleary-eyed, but satisfied that they had made a big step in their investigation.

The message in newspaper clippings cleared the two laborers of any guilt.

Agatha had once read a book about Egyptian curses. The curse of Tutankhamen was the most famous, and many *fellahin* refused to work on tomb excavations because of such superstitions. Obviously the two poor laborers had fled the camp in a hurry, without telling a soul, because they were terrified by the curse.

So they hadn't stolen the tablet.

There was only one possible conclusion: the precious find was hidden somewhere in the camp.

"You need to keep the three scientists away from base camp as long as possible," Agatha told Chandler. "If we can find out where the tablet is hidden, we'll also discover who stole it, right, Dash?"

"Um . . . what?" said Dash, still half asleep.

"Certainly, Miss Agatha," responded the butler, tying a neat Windsor knot in his tie.

It was 7:25 a.m.

They went to the kitchen pavilion. Dr. Dortmunder was serving breakfast to the other two scientists, who sat at the plank table. He wore a funny Bavarian apron around his broad waist.

"Black coffee and chocolate doughnuts," he

said with a laugh. "We'll need a truckload of energy to face today's mission!"

Dr. Paretsky looked disgusted. "In Poland, breakfast consists of an omelette, kielbasa sausage, and pickles," he commented sourly.

Maigret gulped down his cup of *café au lait* and went off to talk to Jafar. "While we're gone, he'll be in charge of base camp security," he explained.

The Mistery cousins exchanged knowing glances.

By the time Professor Maigret returned, Chandler had already started the jeep's engine. Paretsky sat tall and straight. Dortmunder had his rifle ready. Although he wished he was holding a family-size tub of pistachio ice cream instead.

"Ready," announced Maigret, climbing into the jeep. "See you later, kids!"

"Bon voyage!" Agatha called to him. "Be careful," she said to Chandler.

He nodded and stepped on the gas. The jeep skidded on the gravel and took off in a cloud of dust.

"Now it's all up to us!" Agatha exclaimed after Jafar had headed back to camp.

"How are we going to pull this off?" asked Dash. "We have to make sure Jafar's out of the way. And the rest of the workers."

"You're right," she said. "First let's go down to the dig and make sure they're all busy. Then we can search the rest of the camp for clues."

And that's what they did. Dash used his heat sensor to make sure that the whole crew was accounted for.

Some of the laborers split rocks with their pickaxes and others carried up buckets filled to the brim with crushed rock. Jafar sat at a long counter, sifting through rock fragments, peering at them with a jeweler's magnifying eyepiece and carefully labeling samples for further analysis.

Several more laborers carted off the discarded material, piling it onto a mound a short distance away from the cordoned-off quarry.

"Good morning, Mr. Jafar," said Agatha. "How's it going?"

"Same as usual," sneered the excavation director. "Nothing of interest."

"Dash and I have the whole day free. Would you like some help?"

"Read that sign," he snapped, not even bothering to meet her eyes. "Authorized personnel only."

Agatha feigned deep disappointment. "Oh, too bad! I was so hoping to learn more about your noble profession. It's so fascinating."

Jafar looked up, stroking his pointy beard as he stared at them. The jeweler's loupe magnified

his right eye, making his hypnotic gaze even stranger. "Maybe after lunch I can give you a couple of tips," he conceded. "But you must run off now and let me attend to my work."

"Oh, thank you, Mr. Jafar," Agatha said happily. "That's super nice of you!"

Frowning, he squinted at her through the eyepiece.

Dash and Agatha hurried away. "Cool," Dash said under his breath. "He won't be back at the camp until noon at least. We're on our own."

"Exactly," said Agatha. "Where shall we start? Jafar's tent or the pavilion?"

"At school, they taught us to rule out the long shots first," said Dash. "That Jafar guy gives me the creeps. So I vote for the pavilion."

"Bedrooms or lab?"

"Let's check out their rooms while we know they're away."

They entered the pavilion, eyes wide with curiosity. It was the first time they'd been in the main tent alone. Skipping the kitchen, they went right to the sleeping quarters.

The space was divided into thirds by woven reed dividers; there were three cots, three nightstands, and three wardrobe trunks.

Agatha shot her cousin a questioning look. "So what would your teachers tell us to do next?"

"Always search the most ordinary places first." Dash grinned. "Are you checking to see if I dozed off in class?"

"A little refresher course never hurts!"

They checked under the beds, finding nothing but sand. They patted down all the bedding and pillows. No luck. Then they opened the wardrobe trunks, checking to see that there were no false bottoms.

Still nothing.

"It would be pretty hard to hide a clay tablet

in here," said Agatha. "But we might turn up some clues."

Dash looked through the drawers. In Maigret's nightstand, under a pile of papers, he found an old revolver, well oiled and loaded. "What a weird-looking gun," he said without touching it. "You take a look, you're the expert."

Agatha carefully picked it up with a handkerchief, to avoid leaving fingerprints, and examined it.

Dash knew what she was about to say. "Let me guess. Does it have to do with a memory drawer?" he asked wryly.

She smiled, playing along. "If my memory serves me correctly, this is a World War Two German Luger," she observed. "There's an encyclopedia of firearms in the Mistery Estate library. Maybe the professor collects antique guns."

"It's the first suspicious thing we've turned

up," said Dash. "Why would Professor Maigret need a gun? It could mean he's up to no good . . ."

Agatha nodded, replacing the gun in the drawer in the exact same position and covering it with the pile of papers.

They spent another half hour rummaging through the three professors' possessions, reading their notebooks, letters, and official contracts. Then they went to the laboratory.

It was the biggest space in the pavilion, chock-full of books, computers, and equipment used to analyze archaeological finds: microscopes, electronic scales, centrifuges, infrared lamps, and a stash of syringes, pipettes, tweezers, and chemical reactants.

"I'll check out the cupboards," Dash suggested.

"Good idea," said Agatha, surprised he was taking the lead. Though it *was* his exam, after all. "Be careful not to leave any traces."

They each took a pair of sterile gloves from a box on the workbench.

Ever since she was little, Agatha had loved playing in her parents' lab, so she knew quite a bit about analytical testing. It seemed that every machine in this lab had been turned off after the tablet was stolen. There were a thousand chemical clues to collect, but they'd need more time to do the search justice.

Just before noon they stopped to compare notes.

"Did you find anything?" asked Dash. "I've got zero."

"Nothing yet. It would take years to examine all this."

"But we've just got a day and a half. Then they flunk me," Dash said gloomily.

Agatha tried to comfort him. "Look on the bright side. If there's nothing here, that means

it's more likely we'll find something in Jafar's tent . . ."

"Okay, let's keep going!"

Agatha put her plastic gloves in her pocket— it wouldn't be safe to leave them in the trash can—and started to follow him out of the lab. On the threshold, she turned to call Watson.

The cat was curled up on the workbench. In the bright midday sun, she could see that his white fur was covered in dust.

"Wait, Dash!" she exclaimed. "I've got an idea!" She grabbed the infrared lamp and put it on the workbench. When she pressed the switch, Watson jumped up and ran under the counter, his tail bushing out.

"What are you doing, cousin?"

"Why didn't I think of this earlier?" Agatha said. "The tablet sat here on the bench for a whole day!"

"So what?"

"The infrared lamp can detect individual particles of clay," she explained. "Look!"

A light dust appeared on the workbench, the same shape as the tablet they'd seen in the photograph.

Agatha raised her arms in victory. "Yes!"

Without wasting a minute, she drew some dust into a syringe, transferring it into a small vial in the centrifuge. "This will tell us the exact chemical composition," she said, satisfied.

"Why do we need to know that?" Dash asked, bewildered.

"To find the tablet, dear cousin!"

When the centrifuge stopped, a sequence of numbers appeared. Dash's face brightened. "You're a genius, Agatha!" he said, taking out his EyeNet. He quickly scrolled through the menu. "I just have to find the right function!"

When he was ready, Agatha carefully read the sequence of numbers, and he keyed them in. Then they left the pavilion, keeping an eye on the EyeNet's monitor as they waited for a signal.

Dash crisscrossed the site, followed closely by Agatha. At long last, as they were approaching the quarry, the EyeNet gave an unmistakable *BEEP!*

"To the quarry!" shouted both Mistery cousins.

They broke into a run. The hot sun was high overhead, and all the workers sat in the shade eating lunch, except for Jafar, who was scrutinizing a pebble through his loupe with intense concentration.

The two young detectives crept through the site. Ducking from tent to tent, they moved quickly and did their best to stay hidden from view.

Dash checked the EyeNet again, setting

the signal to VIBRATE mode. It was coming from
the mound of discarded stones. Perfect—they
wouldn't have to cross the barbed wire.

Unnoticed, they reached the far side of the
mound.

"The tablet is somewhere under this rock
pile. Start digging!" Dash whispered. He set his
Eyenet on the ground and sank his hands into
the crumbled rocks, digging hole after hole.
Panting with heat and exhaustion, he turned to
face Agatha, who was sitting stock-still with the
EyeNet in her hands.

"Why aren't you helping?" he asked.

Agatha looked upset. "Dash, look at the EyeNet," she whispered, passing it to him.

He gazed at the screen and fell silent instantly. The pattern of clay particles was spread out all over the mound, in an area far too large for a tablet.

"It must have been pulverized," Agatha said. "The tablet we're looking for doesn't exist anymore. Somebody destroyed it."

Dash slumped back, staring up at the blazing sun. "That's it, then. The end of the investigation," he said with a bitter sigh. "And the end of my brilliant detective career."

They sat for a moment in silence.

Then, out of the corner of his eye, Dash saw Agatha pick something out of the rubble. It looked like a long waxy string. Then she picked up several more.

"Did you notice these candles?" she asked. "They've been burned the wrong way."

"Huh? What do you mean?"

"The wick is intact, but the wax has been melted away."

Dash picked up one of the candle stubs with its long wick. "That must be some kind of Egyptian custom," he said without interest. "They do everything backward here."

Agatha looked at him. "What did you just say, Dash?"

"That everything's backward in Egypt," he repeated impatiently.

Agatha slapped her hand to her forehead, as if she were swatting a bug.

"Of course! You just answered the riddle!"

Cactus Power

At that exact moment, the jeep Chandler was driving had started to swerve, buffeted by the fierce winds of a sandstorm. They were speeding away from the tiny oasis of Abu Sidan, on the far side of the towering cliffs. Chandler and the three Egyptologists had stopped at the palm grove long enough to search every inch of the solitary brick building, the tumbledown shacks, and even the well.

There was nobody there.

"The thieves must have escaped," Dr. Dortmunder said angrily. "We've come all this way for nothing!"

That was exactly the point, Chandler thought. Suppressing a private grin, he arranged his features to look disappointed. "I suggest we head back to the base camp to gather new satellite images," he said gravely.

But on the way back, a howling wind blew out of nowhere. The sand swirled so high that it obliterated the view of the road and the mountains behind.

Suddenly Professor Maigret lurched forward. "Watch out for that boulder, detective!" he shouted.

In the backseats, Paretsky and Dortmunder instinctively covered their faces, sure they were about to smash into the boulders obstructing the road.

Instead, Chandler swerved around the obstacles like a professional race-car driver, which he'd been for a while between boxing and butler school. "Don't worry, gentlemen," he said

in his gravelly voice. "We'll be safe once we get to the ridge."

Just as he predicted, the storm's fury abated as soon as they reached the foothills, and an hour or so later, the jeep drove back through the funnel entrance between the stone cliffs and parked in front of the tent pavilion.

It was sunset, and a gentle breeze blew through the sheltered camp.

As they climbed out of the jeep, the Egyptologists were still coughing and brushing the sand from their clothes.

"Did you find the tablet?" Agatha asked eagerly. "And the thieves?"

"Mission failed," grumbled Paretsky. "There wasn't a living soul at the oasis."

The other two scholars just sighed.

Agatha's face fell. She looked every bit as disappointed as Chandler had, then turned toward him to drop a quick wink.

"The villains escaped," Chandler said, grim-voiced. "I'm going to contact the agency for additional satellite imaging, so we can track their movements."

"Have some dinner first," urged Agatha. "You must all be starving, and Dash and I made an incredible pizza!"

Dr. Dortmunder looked much happier. So did the other two scholars, as soon as they caught a whiff of garlic, basil, and tomato sauce drifting out from the kitchen. All three of them hurried back to their rooms to change out of their sandblasted clothes.

The second they left, Agatha, Dash, and

Chandler went into a huddle. Agatha filled him in on their findings, and asked him where the guns were.

"They're still in the jeep, Miss Agatha," he replied. "Would you like me to get them?"

Just at that moment, Professor Maigret burst into the kitchen. "Get what?" he asked suspiciously.

Dash bent over the oven, pretending to check on the pizzas, while Agatha quickly thought up an excuse.

"Dessert!" she said, smiling. "We've prepared a surprise dessert!"

In a way, this was perfectly true.

She and Dash had spent the entire afternoon laying a trap to catch the culprit red-handed.

Maigret surveyed the fully set dinner table with a frown. "Why have you set an extra place?" he asked.

Agatha kept her voice level. "We've asked Mr.

Jafar to join us tonight, if it's all right with you," she explained.

The professor eyed her suspiciously, then said, "Fine with me."

Agatha exhaled in relief and went to help Dash with the pizza cutter. Paretsky and Dortmunder sat down, and then Jafar arrived. Looking tense, he perched on the edge of his folding chair.

"Buon appetito!" said Agatha cheerfully as Dash passed out slices of pizza. But instead of eating her own, she furtively observed the behavior of her fellow diners. Professor Maigret cut his into neat triangles with a knife and fork. Dr. Paretsky frowned, scraping off the top layer of cheese. Dr. Dortmunder folded his slice in half so he could eat twice as fast, while Jafar barely nibbled the edges, careful to keep the sauce out of his beard.

Dash and Chandler ate their slices the usual way, but they both looked a little bit nervous.

When all four suspects had finished their meal, Agatha stood up.

The moment of truth had arrived.

"Ahem," she said, clearing her throat.

"Something wrong?" Dr. Dortmunder asked kindly as he loosened his belt. "Bit of pizza crust down the wrong pipe?"

"Dear sirs," she began, "I must tell you exactly what happened on the fateful night that the tablet was stolen."

Maigret almost knocked over his glass of Bordeaux. "Now the children are playing detective?" he sneered.

Agatha paused momentarily, glancing at Chandler and Dash, who both nodded that she should go on.

"Our story begins in the afternoon three days ago, when the tablet was brought to the laboratory for cleaning," she stated. "While Dr. Paretsky began to translate the inscription,

rumors spread through the camp that the strange hieroglyphs were backward. Some of the workers were frightened, and started to whisper about the pharaoh's curse."

"By Anubis, how could you know about that?" interrupted Jafar, looking terrified.

Agatha ignored him, pressing on with her speech. "That evening, two of them went to their tent and found a note that filled them with terror," she continued, her confidence growing. "Before evil could strike them, they fled from the camp, climbing over the cliffs to avoid getting caught at the checkpoint."

"That's ridiculous!" snorted Dr. Paretsky, enraged. "Those two men robbed us!"

Agatha shook her head, holding up the incriminating note. "My dear sirs, this message was left in their tent by one of the four of you!"

The scholars jumped out of their chairs, eyeing each other warily.

"How can you be so sure?" Dortmunder demanded.

"Somebody wanted to make them look guilty, dear doctor," Agatha replied calmly. "Now let's jump forward. Late that night, worn out from a long day at work, you all retired to your rooms. One of you, however, did not go to sleep. He waited until the camp was quiet, then collected the tools for his sinister plan." She turned toward Maigret. "For security, he took a gun with him."

"What gun are you talking about?" exclaimed the elderly Egyptologist.

"Perhaps your own Luger, Professor?" replied Agatha. "But that's not the point," she continued. "The mysterious man crept down to the quarry, to the mound of discarded stones. The perfect place to ensure that no one would ever find the tablet."

She paused for a breath, her eyes narrowing.

"The man took out the candles he'd brought with him, melting the wax. He poured the hot liquid into the crevices formed by the hieroglyphs, creating a cast of the tablet. Now the inscriptions were reversed, making it easier to decipher . . ."

"That's insane!" cried Maigret. "You could do the same thing with a computer or even a mirror!"

"That's exactly the point, Professor," Agatha said with an angelic smile. "The mysterious man wanted to erase those inscriptions forever so no one could do the same thing. In fact, as soon as the wax cooled, he pounded the tablet to dust. Then he hid the copy in the one place where he could preserve it, a place where the wax wouldn't melt. It's very hot here in Egypt, you know . . ."

Just then, Dr. Dortmunder sprang to his feet and drew the Luger from his belt. Evidently he'd taken it from Maigret's nightstand before coming

into the kitchen. "Stay where you are," he ordered, backing in small steps toward the freezer. "I don't know how you managed to uncover my secret, but now we'll have to do things the hard way!"

"Dortmunder?!" Maigret was stunned. "Is what she said true?"

"Of course, Professor. Do you think I'm an idiot?" Dortmunder snarled. "I know the way these things go. You're the team leader. As soon as you locate the pharaoh's tomb, you would take all the credit for the discovery and no one would even remember my name. Or yours, Paretsky, you spineless fool!"

Chandler was grinding his teeth, ready to throw one of his knockout punches. Agatha placed a hand on his arm, as Dortmunder pointed the gun at him. "Not one step closer," he threatened.

Dash trembled in shock. None of this had been

part of their plan. The situation was spiraling out of control.

Agatha took a deep breath. "Calm down, Dr. Dortmunder," she said firmly. "Take the cast out of the freezer and leave in the jeep. I promise, nobody will follow you!"

Dash broke out in a cold sweat.

What was his cousin saying? Had she lost her mind?

"I accept your offer, Miss Nosy." Dortmunder's chuckle had a nasty edge. "Everyone against the wall! Shut up and stand still!"

He pulled a rope from a shelf and flung it at Dash. "Tie yourselves together, nice and tight!" He raised the Luger.

The others obeyed. Dortmunder took a step backward, slowly opening the freezer door.

Chandler shifted his weight.

"Don't try any tricks!" the scientist threatened them, nervously waving the gun.

Without taking his eyes off his prisoners, Dortmunder reached one hand into the freezer, unpacking box after box of ice cream. Finally he got to the bottom, where he had hidden the wax cast.

"Ouch!" he cried suddenly. "What just pricked me?"

He grimaced in pain, then froze in place, eyes wide open and gun pointed, paralyzed by the *petrificus* toxin.

Freeing her wrists from the rope, Agatha

brought it over to tie up the culprit. "Your turn to shut up and stand still!" she said cheerfully, pinching his motionless cheek.

"What happened to him?" exclaimed an incredulous Professor Maigret. "It looks as if he's been mummified!"

Dr. Paretsky slumped into a faint, and Jafar started to pray in a tremulous voice.

Dash and Chandler ran to Agatha, elated. Without her brilliant idea, they would never have gotten through this alive.

Agatha grinned at Dash. "You see, Agent DM14?" she said with a twinkle. "We solved the riddle of the pharaoh!"

Mystery Solved...

On the crisp desert dawn, Agatha and her companions saddled their camels for the return journey. Maigret and Paretsky stood in front of the pavilion, looking relaxed for the very first time.

The two scholars had stayed up well past midnight, taking detailed photographs of every last hieroglyph on the wax cast.

"It will take time—might be months, even years—but you can count on us. We're going to find the hidden entrance to the pharaoh's tomb!" Once again, the elderly Frenchman's voice had the energy of a much younger man.

"I can't wait to read the headlines!" beamed Agatha.

Jafar joined them, his cotton robes flowing. He gave each of the investigators a small amulet of the jackal-headed Anubis. "For protection against bad luck," he explained.

As the three of them put on their amulets, Chandler thanked him with a solemn nod.

The only one missing was Dr. Dortmunder. He had been handcuffed before the *petrificus* toxin wore off, and as soon as he came to, he started complaining that he was starving. The others had taken turns feeding him ice-cream pops, which he could eat with his hands cuffed behind his back. Soon the police would be coming to take him away.

Agatha wondered if the arresting officer

would be the same man Dash had pretended to shoot for the BBC. If so, she hoped they'd take pictures.

As they were about to leave, Professor Maigret reached out to shake Chandler's hand. "Thank you again, detective," he said, his eyes shining. "I've reported your excellent work to Eye International. I didn't quite understand their response, but they seemed very satisfied."

"What did they say?" Dash straightened up anxiously.

"Something about an exam."

"Uh-oh!" Dash frowned. "Anything else?"

"I believe the phrase they used was 'Aced it.'"

Dash broke into a grin. "Excellent news, Professor Maigret!"

The three adventurers bid good-bye to the scientists and started their long journey back.

This time, Dash was the one boldly taking the

reins and urging his camel to gallop. Finding out that he'd "aced" the exam had made him feel like a superhero.

When they reached the top of the ridge, he stopped to admire a panoramic view: the great green banks of the Nile with its colossal monuments, the cruise ships and graceful *feluccas* sailing along the great river, the temples of Karnak and Luxor, swarming with tourists.

Agatha pointed a finger at his chest. "You've got a call," she said.

"Huh? What?" he replied, coming out of his daydream.

"Your EyeNet is ringing!" his cousin repeated.

Dash looked at his EyeNet, which was vibrating, flashing a rainbow of lights. "What do they want now?" he wondered. "I thought the exam was all finished."

He brought the device to his ear, speaking in a

professional tone. "Agent DM14 at your service."

He listened for a few seconds, looking blank-faced, then started to stammer. "Oh no, it's not a wrong number. It's Dash . . . yes, I'm sorry, I thought you were joking!"

Agatha and Chandler both looked at him, questioning.

"It's for you," said Dash, passing the EyeNet to Agatha. "It's your mother. She sounds pretty mad!"

The girl raised an eyebrow and spoke. "Hello, Mommy."

Chandler blushed red as a beet.

"What are we waiting for, guys?" called out an exuberant Dash. "Let's beat them to London!" He spurred his camel forward with a slap on its rump, but instead of surging ahead, the animal started to lean to one side, listing farther and farther until it hit the ground with a thud, playing dead.

Agatha and Chandler's laughter echoed through the Valley of the Kings.

Agatha's next mystery . . .

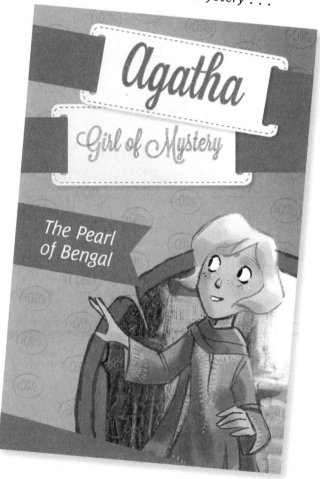

Agatha

Girl of Mystery

The Pearl
of Bengal